Kevin The Vampire

Kevin The Vampire

A Novelette

WILL MADDEN

SQUARE STRAW PRESS

Nashville, TN

ISBN 978-0-9981404-2-1
Square Straw Press
Nashville, TN

To everyone out there who has ever dreamed
bigger than all the world: your ambitions are
psychotic, and with God as my witness, I shall
think about stopping you.

CONTENTS

1. The Organ Man

H E LAY STRETCHED OUT across the altar on his back. His knuckles rested against the cool marble above his head, hands thrown up in a gesture of surrender. But the nails were razor sharp, the fingers could clench into a fist harder than granite. *Options always remain, no matter how hopeless it seems.* Kevin wasn't giving up. Not yet.

But what use were hands against so godly an adversary? The light of a hundred candles danced across the chiseled chest that loomed above, the stony eyes scrutinizing him with almost merciless pity. *It is finished,* they seemed to say.

But the meek of this earth have their fill of nothing.

Whatever happened, Kevin wouldn't be the first to blink.

Here in the nave of this abandoned church, he and the figure hanging on the wall were having a staring contest.

This promised to kill the better part of the evening. As sculpture and vampire, neither tended to blink unless they were up to mischief.

Kevin liked a challenge.

"Jesus Christ!" he shouted suddenly. "What do you think of my nail polish?" He held up a hand for inspection.

No luck. The murdered messiah did not break eye contact.

"You love everything anyway," Kevin muttered.

But this time, the son of God was right, it was a nice shade. Not the lustrous black like he'd worn in the 80s: he'd traded that in for an actual color, some kind of greenish blue. The first time you see it, you think *Meh*, but then you realize it's an elegant choice. He checked the bottle that lay at his side. Teal Killer

Sunrise, it was called. $2.99 at Walgreens. The only thing open in this podunk Ohio town after sunset.

Let new vampires do half capes and face powder, studded leather. Topknots and Nirvana tees, whatever vamp kids were up to these days. At some point, you had to settle into yourself.

Like the name. Kevinus sounded cool with the accent on the second syllable but looked dumb in print. He'd tried dozens of permutations: Cevinus. Qehveenoz. Kuh-V-noose. It was all a wreck. *I'll stick with Kevin, thank you.*

When he first got turned, Kevin called himself Gaius Severus because it was badass and Latinate names were chic at the time. But the undead he ran with shortened it to Guy, and if you are going to answer to that you might as well just be Kevin.

Once upon a time, he'd sated his appetite for blood and brawling in the drug-fueled, fast-living City of New York. When the drop in the crime rate ruined the party, he skipped town to terrorize rural America under the guise of a door-to-door salesman.

Somewhere along the way, riotous Gaius Severus reverted to ol' Kevin.

To avoid the Big Bright End one morning, he stumbled into an open grave in the cemetery of St. Agnew's, an abandoned church in a small town an hour outside of Dayton. The next night he broke into the chapel just to sample the local color. It was small and cozy, with an authentic stench of decayed sanctimony. Inside the sacristy, he found all sorts of holy doodads which he spent the next week setting in recesses around the church, arranging and rearranging until it struck the right notes of mockery, piety, and despair. He lit maybe a billion candles. The atmosphere reminded him of being cursed by God to live forever, a scorn which suffused his limbs with warmth, like a hot toddy after shoveling the driveway in the wake of a winter storm.

Now that his butt could no longer go numb, sitting the last pew of a church was one of the best places to examine his thoughts—which amid agelessness was practically a form of hygiene. A few miles away, a train transporting car- after car- after carload of coal blew its whistle all night long like nobody was left on the continent to hear it. Kevin liked that. Sometimes he'd sit with the paper, reading the news, scouting pictures of locals for something tasty. A pity how in the little town, everyone subsisted on nothing but Kentucky whiskey and high-fructose sweetener. God's real curse, he mused, was for him to eat cornblood forever.

Whenever he felt vampirism weighing him down, he'd mount the chancel and drape his body across the altar. Kevin always took off his shoes when he did this. He had no idea why. Pretty much his entire life was a sacrilege now. He'd smeared lewd paintings with human blood on the walls! After that, how could either he or God care about some schmutz on the dinner table? But Kevin felt there always had to be a line that separated you from barbarians, and this is where he drew his.

Plus the crucified Christ was the only one to whom he could show off his brightly colored, hand-knit socks.

Lying on the altar was also the only comfortable way to contemplate the mural of the Assumption on the ceiling. He studied Mary carefully, her head encircled in a golden nimbus, her eyes lifted beatifically. Her feet tread clumsily on the faces of the apostles below, who seemed to be shoving her bodily up into paradise.

Heave! God Almighty left his own mother behind like an iPhone charger! But no worries, we'll make it right. On three, all ye disciples. One, two. Heave!

He couldn't say why, but over time this started to feel like a scene from his own life.

Slaughtering people and gaping at religious art tied the extremes of Kevin's life together nicely: on one hand action and blood, on the other quiet and meditation. He might even think himself happy if not for the cornblood month after month, year after year.

Some nights he sat in the presence of just a candle or two. On others, he lit so many, it felt like the room was on fire.

Remember light, remember day? Did he want to?

Yes. Part of the joy of owning a great painting is contemplating the price you paid for it. For Kevin, life as a vampire was a special work of art.

On other occasions he reflected on Gaius Severus, svelte and handsome, raising hell outside punk rock clubs like CBGBs. He did this the way you sometimes think about the lives of people you learn about on tv.

He'd managed to get the church organ working again. Organ repair and maintenance: the verbal irony appealed to him. Over the years he'd taught himself to play. Bach was beyond him, so he contented himself with popular tunes, particularly Billy Joel. "Organ Man" had both a sinister and self-mocking ring to it.

> *Suck out my spleen, you're the organ man*
> *Eat off my face tonight*
> *We all got some food in our artery*
> *And you've got us bleedin' . . .*

He had eternity to work on it.

Kevin had eaten two hundred forty-three people. All that killing ought to have made him remorseful or filled him with sado-maniacal glee, but he felt no different about any of these meals than the hamburgers he had eaten while human. To an extent, he enjoyed outwitting his prey—it was smarter than hamburger anyway—but Kevin was superfast, superstrong, and mostly immortal. The thrill had dissipated. Once, he had worn a cape, held out his arms towards his victim, and said "Bleh blah bloh." The old gentleman had tried to give him the Heimlich maneuver. Since then, he could no longer be bothered with the theater of the kill. Yes, people tasted better with adrenaline in their system, so if you were a gourmet, it paid to scare them a bit, but lately Kevin had taken to eating them dry, like oatmeal out of the canister. Time wasted toying with his food could be better spent lying on the altar in his stocking feet, staring up at the crucified god on the wall and feeling a little down on himself.

2. The Hunter

ONE EVENING KEVIN headed over to the Walgreens. He wanted to pick up some red food dye for the baptismal font, Windex for the stained glass, trash bags for the fallen leaves in the churchyard, and—let's see how it goes—maybe take a look in the cosmetics aisle to see what's passing for glamor here at earth's end.

An hour later, Kevin walked out with two bottles of polish, a lip balm, and a pack of lemon gummies. He also nabbed a copy of the local paper from the coin machine outside.

Raking leaves. Who was he kidding?

One article in the *Husker* reported that local corn production was up three percent this year. Did you know corn is used in everything from glass cleaner to lipstick?

With exasperation, he turned the page.

Vampire Hunter in Town

Undead be on guard! Unholy abominations beware! Supernatural exterminator, Edvard von Heusen, has promised to liberate our blighted berg from the sanguine predation of our loved ones. Armed with the most pungent garlics and cruciform crosses . . .

Garlic! Kevin crumpled the newspaper and threw it on the ground. Everybody knew from books about vampires that nothing from books about vampires is true.

Still, someone snooping around churchyards was a problem that demanded to be dealt with. Oh, but why did it have to be right now? This was totally the night he was going to get around to tidying up the sacristy.

Alternative lyrics to "Only The Good Die Young" were begging to be born!

Plus, "Edvard von Heusen" sounded like a joke— as if van Helsing had fallen on hard times and was now living out of the back of his truck. Eddie van Housing.

The hunter had probably paid for this news article himself. Likely he was the kind of charlatan who traveled from town to town, digging up graves and mutilating corpses. He'd plant some exotic-looking sigil among the debris, claim he'd killed a vampire, and try to collect a bounty before moving on. A rough gig. Disinterring bodies was hard work, and while many of these rustics believed in vampires, few believed enough to pay a hunter's fee. Kevin guessed this one relied on a side scam, possibly installing supernatural home security systems for widows and schizophrenics.

Kevin despised men like this, but mostly they were just a nuisance. The policy among vampires was to leave them alone. The mysterious disappearance of a so-called vampire hunter only invited scrutiny, so you were supposed to take a nap and give them time to sweep through town.

Meh. Kevin couldn't be bothered with a nap.

Anyways, he decided this news was no cause for alarm. He just took off his boots, lay across the altar, and pondered the apostles trying to hurl the Virgin Mother up into heaven.

She looks so heavy, he thought as he let his eyes rest. *Far too heavy to stand on a cloud.*

Later that night, he was woken by a shuddering knock at the door of the church.

"Yoo-hoo!" sang a voice outside. "Someone home? Can I come in?"

Who is supposed to answer? Kevin thought. *Me or God?*

He folded his arms across his chest and refused to speak. He wasn't afraid of confrontation, he just didn't like how nasally his voice sounded when it echoed inside the church.

The banging sounded again, heavier than before. On the third blow, the wood splintered near the lock and the door swung open.

God damn it, he thought. *I cannot goddamn stand going to Home Depot.*

A figure appeared in the doorway, illuminated by the votive candles Kevin had lit near the entrance. Whoever it was wore a hood.

"I'm looking for uhh." Paper shuffled. It continued shuffling.

O most gracious Virgin Mary. *That's how the prayer goes,* Kevin thought. Ever was it known, that anyone who flew to thy protection. *Flew. I guess that means they got her up there somehow.*

"Gay-us? Gay-us Severe-us?"

Kevin let one of his arms fall from the side of the altar. *I swear to Christ, the rural Midwest!*

"Is that you," the voice asked meekly. "Gay-us? Are you Gay-us?"

I've killed two hundred forty-three people, thought Kevin. *When you come for me, hunt me like a monster—like an animal if you must!—but I will not play your third-grade mind game. Will not!*

Kevin turned his head to study the intruder. He wore a hunter's cloak, the kind he'd only seen in movies where fairy tale children slaughter, like, fifty orcs. A duffel bag was slung over his shoulder, one of the red ones they used to give you for smoking too many cigarettes.

"What nefariousness hazard thou here, demon," boomed the voice suddenly, "lying like a corpse in a house of God? Doest thou not tre-e-e-emble to blaspheme before the Lord, who curses nothing more mightily than thee in all creation?"

Nothing? thought Kevin. *Imagine being a woodpecker, forced to beat a tree with your face every time you got the munchies. Tell me God didn't curse the woodpecker something fierce.*

He might have said this out loud, but he didn't want to degrade himself by being witty.

Perhaps Kevin ought to sit up and face his visitor, a mortal enemy and all, but it seemed too much trouble. The hunter's footsteps approached over the marble titles. He wore fuzzy boots and shuffled. Everything about him shuffled or duffled.

The bag dropped at the foot of the altar stairs and landed with a woody clunk. The hunter fell to his knees and dug through it. Pulling out a garland of garlic, he raised it ceremonially above his head.

Bowing to the tabernacle, he laid it around his neck. Next, he tested the edge of a hand axe. He winced and sucked his thumb before attaching it to his belt. Locating a wooden stake, he clenched it in his teeth as he continued to rummage, strewing the bag's contents everywhere.

Finally, he laid hands on a small wooden cross and raised it menacingly toward the vampire.

Kevin lifted his arm wearily and waved it at the enormous crucifix on the wall behind him.

The hunter shrugged and placed the cross back in the bag.

Eddie van Housing, Kevin reminded himself.

"Uhryer Eyous?"

He spat out the stake. "Are you Gay-us?" With a gloved hand, he fished clumsily at a wood sliver left on his tongue. "Mehk! Gay-us. That's you, right?"

"Are you gonna slay me or cook a pizza, garlic man?" Kevin snapped.

He chastised himself for breaking his own rule.

Suddenly the hunter's countenance darkened, and

his anger seemed to summon wind. Fire blazed in the eyes as his chest swelled.

"At the hands of man and before the eyes of God, the time has come to face judgment! Here I hold a list. Two hundred twelve? thirteen names . . . whose souls call out for the impalement of your never-beating heart. Therefore! For the third time, I ask you—and so help me, this time I'll be answered!—Are. You. Gay-us. Severeli-us?"

Fuck my life, thought Kevin. *All right, let's get this done.*

Swinging his body up on the altar, Kevin crossed his legs and cupped his chin in his hand. His tongue teased the tip of a hooked incisor as a wicked smile crossed his face.

"But you can call me sweetheart."

The hunter vanished in a dark blur as he rushed the stairs. A hand struck Kevin's throat with enough force to carry him back over the altar. On the fall to the ground, the vampire twisted the stake loose, but von Heusen's limbs surged with superhuman strength. The two wrestled across the apse, hand-to-hand, body-to-body. Equally matched, they snarled, striking and countering with ferocious speed and power.

Over a long struggle, one of the combatants began to flag.

Kevin pinned the hunter on his stomach and sunk in his teeth hard behind the neck.

It was like chomping down on a piece of wood.

The hunter rolled onto his back, clenching his heaving stomach as merry tears streamed down his face.

Kevin swiped a silver candleholder from the altar and beat his attacker mercilessly about the head, but the other's undead laughter never faltered for an instant.

3. The Adventurer

WHEN KEVIN HAD EXHAUSTED his rage on the hunter's face, he placed the bent candlestick back on the altar and helped him to his feet.

"Who are you?" he demanded.

The vampire smiled, fangs extended. "Don't you recognize an old friend, Gaius? It's me, Grackle."

Kevin studied the face. He had known Grackle well during his early days, his Gaius Severus days, but if he hadn't been told, Kevin might never have recognized the vampire standing before him.

"It's true, I've changed a little. I've been everywhere since we met last. Seen everything. Not everything.

Lots of ticks left on my checklist, but very few involve the insides of rural churches. I've eaten more than cornblood, I'll tell you that."

Kevin hopped back up on the altar to distance himself from the old cloak Grackle wore. Its stench had no place in a house of God, no matter how defiled!

Still, it was good a see a familiar face. The two had been friends in New York, to the extent Gaius Severus could stand other vampires.

The newcomer tilted his head up toward Kevin. "Say 'Hello, Grackle. Been a long time, Grackle. How are you, you old scoundrel?'"

Kevin crossed his feet over his thighs into a lotus pose. His socks were truly ridiculous.

Grackle sighed. "The saying goes: vampirism would be perfect if not for the vampires. You have two sorts. First, the young ones who want to suck everything dry without knowing how to enjoy a drop. But the shortcomings of children you learn to forgive. At some point they become the other kind: bored aristocrats, ensconced in the cultural high ground of evil, but feeling murder is beneath them. Has that happened to you yet, Gaius? If I ask around about you, will I hear that's what you've become?"

Kevin knew Grackle had already done his asking around. If he'd been able to find out anything from the locals, he needed to learn what it was.

The elder vampire continued. "Most of our kind barely skim the potential of the gift we've been given. I've seen the world from vantage points few would dare. Where no mortal can tread and hope to survive. The rim of a volcano about to explode, for instance: the heat, the smoke, the raw glow of molten stone. Magnificent!"

Magmificent, thought Kevin.

"I've climbed dizzying rock faces with just my claws and fangs. The intoxication of those seductive heights, every limb in my body shivering with the temptation to let go. Oh, you cannot imagine the thrill of finally surrendering to that impulse, the delicious fall a thousand feet and more—down onto jagged rock, the rare mountain air forced into my dead lungs on descent. Simply jumping out of an airplane without a parachute doesn't compare—although you should try that too, especially when you plummet directly into a fissure in the earth. Subterranean free-fall. The switch from the atmosphere to below the earth is indescribable. Then, the wait in exquisite agony as your body slowly stitches itself back together. The pain is like a drug opening up new avenues of the mind."

He really is Eddie van Housing! Kevin thought with a giggle.

"It amuses you to lay yourself out like a sacrifice on this altar before the eyes of a dead God—but I challenge you to offer your body to the rude earth of the world's farthest corners, not these pretty," (here he sneered) "artifacts of man's delusions about the infinite. It's true a vampire can neither live nor die, but few have ever made more than a half-hearted attempt at either. Perhaps you've been to Europe? I've walked! Across the bottom of the ocean. Wanna know what the Mid-Atlantic Ridge is like? Go see it yourself! You know how when mortals feel so completely overwhelmed, they claim to feel the presence of God? Like that, it's like that!"

"Why are you here?" Kevin asked. He knew his visitor wasn't on a speaking tour.

Grackle laughed from the belly. "I was wondering if you still knew how to fight. If you can still handle an opponent more powerful than some beefcake gym rat."

"Am I still a beast brawler then?"

"Meh. To be honest, if I were human, I'd fear heart disease more than you. You know, the *silent* killer. Clogged arteries don't play Billy Joel. Hey, you know who hangs out in churches all day? Old people. You've gotten old, Gaius."

"Just Kevin."

"Kevin is the name your human sow gave you. What do you need that name for? Do you want to be human again?"

Kevin hissed.

"Gaius is what you were called back when you meant something. Sure, you were young and stupid—an absolute bore!—but you believed in evil then. You were a child, but a beautiful, vibrant child *of evil*. Now look at you. You really are a Kevin, Gaius."

"Call me Kevin," Kevin repeated.

Grackle frowned. "Never mind falling from

mountains. People, Gaius. Have you ever really spoken to them, found out what they want and dream and fear?"

"Beh. Talking to the meat! Now *you've* gone soft."

"I didn't say pity them. On the contrary. But talk to them. Take the time to get to know everything about them. So you can crush them slowly, completely. Build their expectations sky high, then tear them down brick by brick. Until death becomes truly a mercy. Be a *mercy-giver*, Gaius. There lies the real pleasure of the vampiric life."

"I collect nail polish. The bottles are nice to look at, plus they don't bitch about their feelings. Two things more than I can say for mortals."

"Boring."

"Now, St. Sebastian over there, he and I are tight. I paint him whatever colors I want."

Kevin pointed to a statue of a naked human tied to a tree, arms stretched over his head, body riddled with arrows. The eyes tilted softly upward, supple cupid lips hanging slightly agape, a holy aura encircling the face. The white marble was now a sparkling whirl of pastels and skin tones. Like a superhero sidekick awaiting rescue.

Grackle nodded his compliments, then continued:

"You have to talk to people, Gaius. Death means less to mortals than they think. They have no idea what you're taking from them. They fear you because you emerge from the darkness, the face of a monster on the body of a man. They're afraid of the pain our bite inflicts, though it's sweeter and easier to endure than they imagine. But death? Death doesn't raise a goosebump on them."

"I was human too once. I haven't forgotten."

Grackle sighed. "I'll get to the point. I came looking for you in the guise of a hunter because I wanted to see if you are ready to fight for your life. Because it's come to that. The humans are preparing to exterminate us all, to the very last."

"They tried that in the sixteenth century. Remind me how that went."

"This time they can do it."

Kevin waved a hand dismissively. "A vampire knows how to hide even better than he knows how to kill. They'd never be able to hunt us all down."

"They won't have to. As you know, we can hide from anything but ourselves."

Kevin cocked an eyebrow. "Unless you mean this hunt is philosophical . . ."

"I mean if they get their way . . . " Grackle leaned close enough to the altar to whisper. "We'll be everywhere."

4. They Want To Join Us

KEVIN SLID DOWN OFF the altar. "What do you mean, we'll be everywhere?"

Grackle shrugged. "I mean we'll be everyone. The humans don't plan to hunt us, Gaius. They plan to become us."

Kevin's widow's peak furrowed all the way down to his eyebrows. "All of them?"

"Vampirism is a consumer product now. Or will be shortly. Human scientists have isolated the mutagen that makes us what we are. And they are going to sell it. Market it as a panacea. A cure for cancer, a cure for aging, a cure for a dirty conscience. For rotting teeth, you name it."

"That is too ridiculous to be true."

Grackle smiled, almost delighted to acknowledge it. "Significant side effects, yes, but you can live with them. Forever, it seems. The mutagen will cost no small fortune at first, sold to exclusive clientele at exclusive prices. But once they've gouged the most conspicuous consumption class, they'll have ramped up production enough to start moving down the money tree. Once it reaches suburbia, people will become vampires just because their neighbors are doing it. No one wants to be the only family on the block that isn't immortal."

"Insanity. Who will they all eat?"

"I don't pretend to know. But when the population of undead grows too large, the remaining humans will have no choice but to wage all-out war against us. Too many vampires forced into direct conflict with too few humans. The result can only be disastrous. Lose—well, it's possible—that's anni-hilation. Win, and every remaining drop of human blood will have to be rationed. That probably means civil war. Imagine it, Gaius. Today we eat our fill on the fruit that falls from the tree. Tomorrow, if you manage to survive, you will have to work to the bone for your ration card."

Kevin bared his fangs. "I'd sooner die! So would everyone we know."

Grackle shrugged again. "Everyone will have that choice, of course. In any case, you will not have the luxury of lying on your back staring up at the crucified God and being weary of the world. The way of life you love so much will be destroyed."

The two vampires walked together to the side aisle, where a marble relief showed the living God standing accused and condemned in a court of men. Kevin paused to reflect on the scene. *Give us a share of your immortality,* they cry, *or else assume a share of our death.* Human beings have always been such pricks.

"Besides, it's impossible for them to take the mutagen!" Kevin exclaimed. "Vampires only synthesize it when they desire to turn someone. It cannot be harvested against their will, it cannot even be tortured out of them. The only way the humans could have it is if one of us gives it voluntarily, with the intent of turning the entire human race."

Grackle nodded solemnly. "Have you ever heard of Quercus?"

Kevin was suspicious of Grackle's Latin today. "Coos-coos?" he asked.

"Quercus. As a human, he'd begged Lugurix to turn him. He complained his fellow mortals had become like cogs in a machine. Individuality among men had died out generations ago. Intellectual pursuits were no more than instruments of the most mundane sociopolitical aims, the arts either prestige goods for elites or opiates for the masses. The modern world had placed humanity and *being human* at odds, he said. As a man, Quercus lamented mortal life offered him no freedom except the choice of how to serve the soulless, self-destructive engine humanity had become."

Kevin rolled his eyes. "Bleed me a river," he muttered.

Grackle nodded. "The only escape was vampirism, Quercus believed. As a vampire, he could eat away at the sources of human corruption—the bankers, the advertisers, the journalists, the NFL. Vampirism, he concluded, was the only *humane* action to take. He hoped by draining away humanity's diseased blood, he could restore it to health."

"Like a medieval barber," said Kevin.

"Don't be hard on blood-letters, they paid us a good tithe then. Anyways, Quercus was so ironclad in this conviction, he told Lugurix if he could not become a vampire, he would offer himself as food for vampires, to make stronger the enemies of mankind."

Kevin made a fist, and with a snarl shattered the marble image of Veronica wiping the face of the Lord on the road to Golgotha. "This man was *turned*? If a fanatic like that came to me, I wouldn't stain my teeth on him. I'd cut off his head and let his blood spill on barren sand. There is nothing living or undead to which a man like that isn't an enemy."

"Lugurix was desperate at the time. Hunted, beleaguered, on the run. He needed someone to fight at his side, and he didn't have time to wait for a neophyte to finish struggling with his nature."

"Why not a criminal then? Why this . . . moralizer."

"Although murderers may have no qualms about taking human life, they care no more for our laws than for the humans', at least not at first. Lugurix needed someone who would fall into ranks immediately."

"It was a still a bonehead move."

Grackle chuckled. "Agreed. A malcontent like that is never satisfied. It was only a matter of time before he betrayed us too."

Kevin led Grackle out into the churchyard, where Grackle's clothing would no longer stink up his church. As it was, he would probably have to dip into his dwindling supply of incense.

The two vampires climbed up on gravestones to crouch. Not a thing moved in the nearby wood. The air was stale, the sky a colorless murk. Not even Grackle's news could subtract from the beauty of this sublime Midwestern night.

"When Quercus chose that name," said Grackle, "he swore to be unbending as an oak in his commitment to his ideals. Which I'm sure he has. Whatever his reasons, he has no doubt convinced himself he's acting for the greater good."

"Infuriating!" cried Kevin.

"In any case, Gaius, the fight now falls on us. Quercus is permitting a human corporation to harvest the mutagen from him, and they have developed a plan to exploit it commercially. No option remains. We must destroy Quercus."

"Why hasn't it been done already?"

"He knows the vampires will come for him, so his human masters have hired mercenaries to protect their investment. Quercus has instructed them on our vulnerabilities. Now he lives inside a vault in the basement of a corporate tower at the heart of a major American city. It will take an army to reach him. Can I count on you?"

"Then where are the rest of your vampires? Why have you come alone?"

Grackle paused a moment. "Because right now, there is no one else. The other vampires have refused."

5. Indolence and Inertia

"BUT THAT IS IMPOSSIBLE!" Kevin barked. "Hasn't the Council of Ancients ordered a course of action?"

Breaking off a piece of the headstone he squatted upon, Grackle began sharpening a fang with short, brutal strokes. If Kevin were still alive, the sound of enamel on granite would have made his blood run backward.

"The Council has yet to convene," Grackle said. "A matter this important, the entire body must be wakened, and that might take years. Quercus has advised his corporate masters to act with haste because he knows the response among vampires will be slow."

He punctuated his answer with loud expulsions of gravelly globs of spit.

Cringing, Kevin shielded his eyes from the disgusting behavior. "Hasn't someone told the Mindful Ones of the urgency of the situation?"

"Of course. But the Council has always avoided acting overtly in the affairs of humans. Inertia and indolence have always been the vampires' greatest allies, they argue."

"Surely this merits an exception?"

Out of the corner of his eye, Kevin saw Grackle eating something. No, he was using his newly-jagged incisor to gnaw down his claws! *Revolting*, thought Kevin.

"The procedures and protocols of the Council of Ancients preserve a hierarchy older than writing, and they are extremely time-consuming. But a council member who doesn't receive his due honors risks losing all power and status, so none will permit it. That's why I will act first and let the pieces fall where they may."

Kevin watched Grackle spit claw clippings into the dirt. The end of the world be damned, he needed this disgusting creature out of his sight.

"Grackle, if you declare war on the humans without the Council's permission, you will be branded a criminal. Even if you are in the right, the Council will not brook that kind of insubordination. They will claim they have no choice. The next round of hunters will be for you."

"Ha!" Drawing the axe from his belt, Grackle hurled forth against a nearby monument. The blade clipped the wing of a stone cherub neatly at the shoulder. Grackle roared in triumph.

And now he's destroying the ambiance, thought Kevin.

"Do you mind?" he grumbled. "I live here."

Grackle smiled sheepishly. "It falls within the power of the Council to overlook an independent strike against Quercus even if it cannot condone it."

"It won't do that. Even if you save us all, the precedent set by your action could prove disastrous for the Council. Making examples of the disobedient is how the Council maintains its power."

Grackle grew frustrated. "Letting Quercus upset

the balance between humans and vampires will destroy all we hold dear! So what do you propose I do?"

"It's better to face whatever disaster may come than to be hunted down by our own kind."

"If everyone thinks like that, there is no future, Gaius."

"We're bloodsucking vampires! We thrive on the misery of others. Sacrificing ourselves for the community is not what we do. We glut ourselves on mankind then disappear until the evil we've done is forgotten or becomes legend. We are by nature a *sleeping* evil. That's how we protect ourselves and survive."

Grackle leapt down softly from his headstone. He walked up to the marble cherub he had just mutilated and stared deeply into its pupil-less eyes. He began to caress its cheek. Perhaps the moonlight was playing tricks, because Kevin saw the stone face cringe at the touch. The eyes widened in fear, the lips trembled in a whimper.

Slowly Grackle turned back to Kevin. His expression now seemed slightly drunk.

"You never sleep, do you, Gaius? Sunlight which filters through stained glass cannot turn your flesh to dust, so you sit awake inside that church during the daytime too."

"You're mistaken," Kevin replied.

"Am I?" Grackle pointed a hook-nailed finger. "That lonely grave over there is yours, is it not? The soil hasn't been touched in weeks."

Kevin was silent. *If you told me you were coming over, I might have made the damn bed!*

"This happens among mortals too. The world-weary have great trouble resting. Eventually, they even stop trying to close their eyes."

"Who can afford to sleep? I have so many creative projects. Painting, music—"

"You're not like the others, Gaius. You're only inert and indolent because you lack purpose. If you had something worth dying for, you'd discover something for which to live."

"Who's *indolent?*" snarled Kevin. "Besides, I'm not laying my neck on the block for anyone who refuses to look out for themselves."

"You require a selfish motive: I respect that. You're

not going to do anything for vampirekind. I suppose there's a reason there's no such word."

Kevin drew himself up in his crouch, thrusting back his shoulders. "Whatever bribe you can offer me, you've offered it to the others and they've all declined."

Grackle tilted his head like an inquisitive bird.

"Oh sweet Gaius, you know what I offer. Power. Reputation. Freedom. Whichever you prefer!"

"You are offering me the draconian wrath of the Council of Ancients! No thank you."

Gazing up under a lowered brow, Grackle approached where Kevin crouched upon the gravestone, his footsteps soundless upon the litter of dead leaves scattered across the churchyard. Slowly his arms embraced Kevin's ankles as he rested his head on the inside of his knee. Here was the ancient gesture of entreaty, but from Grackle it seemed like a threat.

Kevin could almost feel the parched lips move as they breathlessly spoke. The voice was so soft, that if not for his supernatural hearing Kevin would not have understood Grackle whisper: "What if I can guarantee you that if we're successful, the Council of Ancients won't take action against us?"

"How could you possibly guarantee such a thing?"

As Grackle stepped back, a thin smile crossed his face. Somewhere in the distance, an owl hooted twice, breaking the unnatural silence on that unholy night.

"Easily. Our first mission will be to destroy the Council."

6. A New Regime

DEEP WITHIN THE SOIL of the nearby wood, the roots of trees strained and snapped as the mighty trunks leaned closer to hear Kevin's response. When he finally spoke, the air crackled and popped with his voice, as if the earth had transformed itself into an amplifier to carry the sound.

"You want to destroy the Council of Ancients? You are out of your mind!"

"Oh Gaius," Grackle sighed sadly. "I would be out of my mind not to. Something more sinister than inertia makes the Council slow to act."

"And what could that possibly be?" asked Kevin.

As he lifted his gaze, Grackle's eyes caught the moon. The reflecting light contorted and throbbed and nearly tore itself apart in the dance.

"Better to reign in hell than serve in heaven. Uncle Miltie said that. The deeper the infernal circle, the more complete the power. During the upcoming war, the Council trusts it can defeat the humans, reduce them to cattle, save the Order of Vampires from annihilation. But the price will be terrible: scarcity of lifeblood will transform the world into a hell for living and undead alike. When that happens, the Council themselves will be like gods!"

"Gods of a wasteland."

Grackle shrugged. "So what? Most people would eat shit if it would make them emperor of the shit-eaters." The idea seemed to please him. "Vampires like you will forge bricks of gold for the ever-more-lavish mausoleums of your betters. You will buy powdered hemoglobin in a plastic bag, which you'll mix with water and heat on a stove. This diet will ruin your eyesight until you'll see an ugly pair of drugstore horn rims floating in every mirror. Nail polish will come in only three colors, one of which will be beige. You will spend all day complaining to the ten vampires with whom you share a tiny mass grave about splinters you got while sanding luxury coffins. The only music you'll have to listen to will be parody versions of jazz standards as performed on *Prairie Home Companion*."

"What? I like those."

"Time will bring you 'round to sanity. And you'll never taste a human being again that doesn't subsist entirely on corn."

"Blech! You really think the Council would invite all that to happen?"

"Hah! In a *heaaaartbeat*," Grackle sang, with an ironic flick of his tongue. "You said it yourself, Gaius: bloodsucking vampires. And while I admire such a deliciously evil plot, I have no desire to fall foul of it. Neither do you. The solution is obvious. Eliminate the Council, and vampires like us will be free to destroy Quercus."

"I don't like it."

An angelic smile crept across Grackle's face. "Of course you don't. You are not a traitor. But this is a critical moment, Gaius. The action—or inaction—we take today will prove the most determinant factor in the course of history, human or vampire."

"Don't look so giddy about it."

Grackle struck his chest with both fists. "But I am giddy! You know how I love to drench my hands in the vitals of things. Honestly, I can't imagine anything more exciting than this—and I was on the Hindenburg!"

"You were not. How did you survive?"

"Most of us did, actually. I blew the airship to cover an embarrassing case of the munchies. But other than my lunch, the deaths were minimal."

"I suddenly feel an ache in my chest I don't understand. Sad? I think the word is sadness."

"Anyways, there's never been a better time to not be alive—in the thick of it, making things happen!"

Enthusiasm is so unbecoming in a vampire, Kevin thought.

"If you fail, they won't kill you," he warned. "Sunlight through pinholes so with every dawn you burn but do not perish. Writhing in Promethean agony until the sun death of the earth.”

That at least, Kevin hoped, was what would happen to Quercus.

Grackle’s dark eye almost seemed to glitter. “You forget there’s no torment of the body I’ve not already willingly subjected myself to: cutting piercing burning freezing bending breaking pressing hammering soaking drying—every fury which almighty nature can inflict. Once I dropped an anvil on my head just to see if my body would accordion, like Wile E. Coyote.”

“You didn’t really need to test that.”

“But it helped me discover ways a vampire mind can overcome outrages against the body. I will teach them to you so that you can fight without fear.”

“Fearlessness can’t help us win an unwinnable battle.”

“The Council’s defenses are rudimentary, Gaius. They believe fear protects them more soundly than any weapon, any wall. For millennia, this has been true! But things change, Gaius. Now there’s us.”

Kevin snorted. “I haven’t said yes.”

"Yet." Grackle leaned toward Kevin, studying him with a squint.

Kevin pondered the name Grackle had chosen. Hardy, resourceful pests. A flock of grackles is called, whimsically enough, a *plague*. Yet Kevin had never heard of anyone inspired with fear at the sight of a grackle.

"As a warrior, you will enjoy fighting at my side. For centuries I've been preparing for this, honing myself into an instrument of will. I've boiled away any doubt that might inhibit my ability to act. I've strengthened my body, I've eliminated every pitfall of the ego, I've dedicated myself to performing this one action perfectly."

"What do you mean, 'for centuries?' Quercus must be younger than I am."

"I mean my chance has finally arrived. Ever since the night I was turned, I've been preparing for an opportunity to destroy the Council of Ancients and assume dominion over the Order of Vampires."

7. A Delicacy of Evil

KEVIN'S EYES NARROWED. "This is all a power grab?"

Grackle's sudden belly laugh startled him. "Of course it is, Gaius! I could have destroyed the Council an age ago. But I had to wait for my chance. A *pretext.* Otherwise, I'd only clear the way to power for whoever could destroy me first. Pshaw! All that for nothing. But if I strike at *this* our most desperate hour, the vampires will stumble over each other to be the first to set the crown upon my brow. I, who acted at the right moment to sweep away a ruling body whose obsolescence threatened us all. Don't like a monarch? Many don't! But who among the undead wouldn't prefer to genuflect to me than to allow our way of life to be destroyed by mortals?"

For all the years Kevin had known him, he had never pegged Grackle for a vampire of ambition. Although at least a millennium old, he still hung out in the nightclubs where the neophytes hunted their prey, letting himself become the butt of jokes, cleaning up the messes of those who couldn't handle the blood alcohol level of their victims. How odd it would it be if Kevin had spent most of a decade foisting the tab on the future king of all the living and the undead.

"Think of what I'm offering you, Gaius. A chance to have fought at my side during the liberation. To serve as part of my inner circle. We few, we . . . *happy* few."

The elder vampire cackled with insidious glee. Did he still intend to let Quercus turn the earth into a food desert? Kevin was hesitant to inquire.

"Why me?" he asked instead.

"Because you hate," Grackle waved his hand, "this. Your little church with its preposterous artifacts and tacky paintings. You hate roosting in the middle of Cornblood, Ohio."

"Plenty of vampires would kill for a place like this!" Kevin exclaimed. "It's a masterpiece of modern unliving. I've everything I've always wanted."

Grackle shook his head sadly. "No. Long ago you believed your strength and daring would carry you along on the current of the upward movers, but the chance has passed you by. While you were striving to make a name for yourself among the fiercest and the evilest, others were becoming the shrewdest. You made the wrong friends—ooh, pity! Now the other vampires have pushed you out."

It was true, Kevin thought. The gang he used to run with had dreamed of turning the underworld on its head. Vampires like Manicheeto, Vitriola, Pope Pius the Nice, Maxilla, and Doctor Popper. They were all ash now, fools who placed too much faith in their own immortality. In the hard times ahead, nobody was left to have his back.

"But you did one thing right, Gaius: you endeared yourself to me. You made the one friend that mattered."

Grackle removed the garland from his neck and, pinching off a few garlic bulbs, lay it upon his head like a crown. He marched around Kevin with regal pomp, humming to himself. Something from *The King and I,* perhaps.

Kevin struck his forehead. "Sweet merciful hell," he cried, "we are defeated before we start."

"Don't be daffy," said Grackle, flapping his arms like a bird. "From this moment, victory is certain. But it was hard, you know: plotting my little coup in plain sight for hundreds of years, memorizing every detail about the Council chambers, learning every routine and procedure. Everything down to the idiosyncrasies of couriers and pages!"

Kevin couldn't imagine the patience such a strategy would require. A thousand years eluding the perception of the most powerful beings on earth. Whose greatest strength is their perspicacity.

As if reading his thoughts, Grackle continued: "Very secretive, the shadowy Council of Ancients. You can't imagine the concentration it took to hypnotize the world's strongest wills to refuse to look at me while I studied them so intently, until I could predict their next move before they knew it themselves. But I have the discipline. All it took was time."

As Grackle smiled, Kevin realized what he found so upsetting about his appearance: you could see both the upper and lower rim of his irises at the same time. It made his gaze seem both gaunt and rapacious.

"I studied you too, Gaius Severus."

With his dirty fingers, Grackle straightened a lock of lustrous black hair that fell past Kevin's ear. He stiffened, but resisted shrinking away from the touch.

"My sweet killer, as your dark power grows ancient, you'll develop the ability to entangle your consciousness with the ones who interest you most, no matter where in the world they are. First, their feelings and moods will come to you in flashes, soon you'll hear snippets of their thoughts, and—if your attraction to them is pure—eventually you'll be able to see them as if you were in the same room. This is how I've followed you, Gaius. This is how I've watched how nobly you bear the hatred of men, the jealousy of God, the bitter ridicule of vampires. With my help, you will become who you were always meant to be. In my name, you will stand resplendent in the robes of kings and receive the tributes owed to the masters of the world!"

Kevin supposed he ought to be upset that Grackle had been psychically stalking him for hell knows how long. But if he thought about it, was it any surprise? His life did possess a kind of poetry. Within his little sanctum, he administered a priesthood to sinister beauty. Someone like him was ideal to contribute an aesthetic to the age of brutality and fear to come. He imagined its victims emitting a gasp of pleasure as they surrendered to despair.

"Why have I brought no others with me, you asked. Because I've come to you first. Why assume I'd prefer another? Do you think your special talents have gone unnoticed by me? That I'm a fool like the rest? You have greatness, Gaius, but you need someone to set it upon a pedestal for others to see. When you stand before a mirror, you see what you truly are: a beautiful evil invisible to everyone. But not to me, Gaius." A sensual, sibilant sigh escaped his lips. "You are a *delicacy* of evil. The world should fall at your feet, *groaning* in appreciation."

Out of the wood came a rumbling. The voices of a

dozen beasts—two dozen, a hundred—began to call out in luxuriant anguish. The most intoxicating music Kevin had ever heard.

"Travesty. A magnificent monster like you, forced to subsist on cornblood, to lie upon an altar in a rundown church like an *exhausted* cliché. It's a crime what they've allowed to happen to you."

Grackle's hand tightened into a fist in Kevin's hair.

"But *one* stroke, *one* action, and it's all undone. Restored to your destined glory. Gaius Severus, before whom even the undead tremble!"

As Grackle whispered in his ear, Kevin felt a tremor in his viscera like a demonic wind penetrating the deepest secrets of sacred precincts, of massive stones falling from the heights of ancient temples.

"Be the first to bow to me, Gaius. I've come to you because you are dying to say yes. What you want most of all is someone to call master. You yearrrrn for someone to free you from the doubt that squanders your potential. Yes! The tingle in your blood that attests I speak the truth. The wait is over. I, Grackle, have planned for every contingency. Wedded to your might, I cannot fail. Everything is completely under my control."

Kevin shoved him away.

"Ha! Not everything. Quercus—much of the outcome still lies with him! And he falls completely beyond your reach!"

Grackle smiled seductively. "Are you sure?"

8. Completely Under My Control

KEVIN LEAPT UP from his crouch upon the gravestone and into a nearby tree. Swinging on an overhanging limb he pulled himself into the foliage where only the angry glow of his eyes could be seen. Grackle trod beneath the branches and stared up patiently, inviting the inevitable question.

"And what influence can you possibly exert over Quercus?"

"A powerful one!" Grackle boomed, the garlics he wore quivering for emphasis. "An ideologue like that will rethink his position a million times, but however often he reaches the same conclusion, he will never act. Not until someone blots out the parts of the picture that don't matter."

"He was your pupil," Kevin hissed.

"In a manner of speaking. If you asked him then, he'd have called me a disgusting creature who did nothing but pollute his ear with revolting lies—a great adversary to both justice and enlightened evil. He believed that too! Quercus always believes, it's his charm. He may yet destroy the whole world, but he's as innocent as a child. And very dear to me."

So that neophyte idiot was Grackle's tool.

It seemed less strange now that the ancient one preferred the company of younger vampires. The Council may have had its secrets and influence, but the youth had numbers. If Grackle could wed his experience to their passion, could anything stop him?

Kevin watched Grackle scratch his scalp, pausing to study something he'd snagged upon a fingernail.

But if Quercus was the example of what happened to those who let themselves be guided by him . . .

The tree's height gave Kevin the advantage of

position but he had no weapon more dangerous than a leafy branch.

"What about his turning?" he shouted down. "The way he approached Lugurix and offered him his throat? His reasons revolt me, but that's not behavior of someone lacking the courage to act."

Grackle licked his lips. "Pretty fortunate timing for Quercus. His petition? A few days sooner or later, Lugurix would have eaten the beating heart right out of his chest. It almost looks as if he were watched over by a guardian angel. Its wings ever so slightly seared."

I didn't say pity the meat. But talk with them. Set their hopes up sky high then tear them down brick by brick until death is truly a mercy.

"What you did was treason, Grackle."

"Conversation, Gaius. Philosophical discussion. In fact, I tried to dissuade him—pointed out paths where he *shouldn't* tread. Down that way, darkness will swallow you whole. It's so much easier to mislead when we tell the truth. I stirred up the righteous anger in him, then *made myself a witness.* To default on his pledge to action would mean betraying his ideologies, not just in his own mind but before me. I would *know*. Twisted, disgusting, debased ol' Grackle would have cause to smile at the hollow boasts, the empty vows. Everything he does now, he does to show me up. Under ordinary circumstances, someone like Quercus would never dare to challenge the entire Order of Vampires—but I taught him to fear my judgment more!"

Grackle swept open his hunter's cloak and set his hands on his hips, displaying the stakes on his belt. And the cut of his checkered flannel pants.

Kevin could feel spikes of contempt being hammered directly into his psyche.

"I regret there's no choice now but to destroy him," Grackle continued. "Of course, it's illegal for one vampire to kill another without a writ from the Council." Grackle rose up on his tiptoes and swung his arms, throwing his weight back and forth. "So I alerted them to his activities via the proper channels. But out of indolence, they did not act! This, naturally, is when I finally became aware of our leaders' ineffectiveness. When I saw it was time for a change."

Grackle swelled with such pride at his cleverness, he began to twitter to himself. Poo-poot, poo-poot!

"I can't believe you consorted with that scum."

The old vampire raised a hand in the beatific gesture depicted on one of the gravestones. "You're harder on Quercus than you ought to be. As a man, he had been friendly, candid, soft-spoken. A mind of genius, as mortal intelligence goes. But his race shat on him, so he turned his back. So strange? Then we vampires treated him no better. In my estimation, his greatest crime is a lack of imagination. Slaughter everyone? Boring. As revenges go, it's the worst."

Crush them slowly, completely. Grackle's earlier words echoed in his mind.

"But I've given Quercus what he wants," he continued. "The timid little man he was, the timid little monster he's become—the only thing he's ever really wanted, although he'd never admit it to himself, is to be feared. Done!"

Grackle gnawed his lip as he giggled. "In the end,

I'm going to give everyone exactly what they want. Some of the Council members have been jealously guarding their power for over five millennia. I've watched it weigh on their minds and torment their sleep. They can't wait to be dethroned. The rest of us? Weary of bowing and scraping to those brutal bastards."

As the cloud cover dissolved above, the light and dark of Grackle's broken smile thrashed and flailed like a demon plowing an angel from behind. "And you, Gaius. What do *you* want?"

Kevin saw now how Grackle had been flattering him the way he wanted to be flattered, pitting each of his fears against the others. This is what he'd done to Quercus, and where was that fool now? Deep in the bowels of some corporate stronghold, strapped in tightly to a machine so the money drip would never run dry. An enemy to every creature living and undead.

I cannot fail, Grackle had said. *Everything is completely under my control.*

Meaning me, Kevin thought. *That must be what he thinks.*

Grackle was planning to throw Kevin under the wheels once the coup succeeded. Or did he expect that having killed the entire Council, he could walk into the forum, his arms covered in ash to the elbow, and expect the vampires to hail him as king? Nobody believes in a disinterested tyrannicide: somebody always, always takes the fall. Who better than Kevin, a virtual unknown, a lunatic assassin whose motivations no one will scrutinize?

And they won't just behead him. The new leadership—perhaps Grackle himself!—would set him on display as an example. Eternally.

Forget it. Live or die, he'd teach the vampire underworld one thing: Kevin McCallister was nobody's patsy!

He felt the cool trace of incisors descend across his lower lip. With a hellborn roar, he leapt from the tree toward Grackle.

9. Decisive Action

KEVIN LANDED noiselessly in front of Grackle, poised to pounce.

"And what are my special talents exactly?" he shouted accusingly.

"Excuse me?" Having assumed a battle stance, Grackle now tilted his head.

"How am I a *delicacy* of evil?" Kevin demanded.

"Hmm? Oh. Al dente. Like a virgin matricide, and—well, look at you. Just as delectable."

"Spare me!" Kevin retreated to his grave, where energy rising from the open earth would replenish his infernal magicks. "Something about this plan I don't like. Murder the entire Council: sure, you seem off-kilter enough to do it. But rule forever in its stead? No, out of character. No king of the world climbs the Himalayas alone in the dead of winter. Or explores the Mariana trench without a submersible. You live for that madness. You'd miss it."

Grackle's body slumped sadly. "Oh, Gaius. Possibly. Who knows, perhaps after we restore stability, I may adventure again. Or I'll cede power to a new Council. A more equitable one. Or more brutal! Hell, perhaps absolute power will corrupt me and I'll rule till Doomsday with an iron fist. Could be fun! What do you say, care to head the secret police?"

Kevin's body seemed to darken into shadow. "What's more you style: slay the assassin, vanish to some remote corner of the globe, cackle in glee over the chaos in which you've left the world behind you."

"If you need assurances—"

"Save your lies! Set up someone's hopes sky high, isn't that right? My special talents, Grackle, what are they? In my day, I was just a brawler, ready to rush into a fight on the smallest pretext. And where did it get me? A few dozen miles outside of Dayton. Gaius Severus may have leapt at the chance to join you, but that moron no longer exists. I refuse this fight. Quercus? The Council? I wash my hands. Do what you will, I leave it to you."

Grackle's face sank with pity.

"You can't, my friend. I'm sorry. Don't you see I've already forced your hand? Should I fail in my attempt, don't you know the vampires will investigate everything I did leading up to my coup? I've spoken to everyone in this town, I'm in the newspaper as a vampire hunter. Why would I come all the way out to your little roost unless it's to recruit you for the operation I'm about to perform?"

Kevin scoffed. "Perhaps you were looking for directions. I helped you find Dr. Bob's house!"

"Hello, my name is Grackle and I'm a hemoholic." His birdish body puffed up with pride. "Only we're overlooking one little detail. This church you squat in, this vampiric wet dream, how do you think you've held such a jewel uncontested for so long?"

"If you had a human's taste, you'd think it's a wreck."

"Oh, would I?" Grackle wrung his hands in delight. "Right now there is a children's theater company trying to use it to stage performances of the Monkey King. They'd have their way too, if not for mysterious financial sponsorship of a movement to preserve St. Agnew's as a historical landmark."

"You don't mean—"

"Of course I do! Your enviable life is made possible from a grant from the Grackle Foundation. Otherwise, tomorrow morning, this place would be shuddering with screams—from delighted corn-fed tots, ages three to eleven."

Too good to be true. Kevin had always thought that, but reassured himself that his superior qualities had made it possible.

"For years now, your sordid little garden has flowered by Grackish waters. My savory taint is all over you!"

Kevin had to turn away from those beady pupils. "I

can't do it. I cannot make war on the Council of Ancients."

"Do you fear having them on your conscience? Of course not, you're a vampire. So be reasonable. I assure you, no Council member would refuse my offer in your place."

Kevin set his jaw. "If I turn you in to the Council, they will reward me. I might not belong to the ruling class when the new order comes, but I'll still hold a rank above the rest!"

Grackle snarled. "Don't be a fool. The Council will destroy you. If I know their vulnerabilities, surely I've discussed them with you. Your knowledge is now a liability."

"What knowledge? You've told me nothing yet!"

The older vampire smiled at youth's expense. "In their place, would you take that risk? Listen, Gaius, this resistance is pointless. Are you really going to help them—help Quercus!—destroy everything you value? You cannot. Then why not fulfill the role I've prepared for you and reap an *embarrassment* of riches?

Trusting me isn't just your only option, it's insanely profitable."

"Trust you? You've taken everything from me."

"I've planned for the future. I've protected my interests—as our kind do! Now protect yours. I'm sorry it came to this, but I leave nothing to chance."

Kevin set his fangs. "Nor do I."

Pulling himself up to his full height, he stretched out his arms. A strong sudden wind tussled his hair. Slowly, Kevin began to levitate.

"Oh dear," sighed Grackle. "Please, please don't."

"I am not your pawn!"

With a flash pop and a cloud of smoke, Kevin vanished. In his place . . .

"You've turned yourself into a bat," Grackle observed sourly.

"I have. And I shall stay this way! I will not play for eternity with a stacked deck. Or should I sacrifice myself for the power grabs of others, to burn but not die in the sunlight for all time, convicted of treason? Madness! I am not your puppet, I am not your *Quercus*!

So let the world reap its due inheritance of blood and ash—now and for all time, I am finished with it!"

"You . . . Holy horrors, Gaius! The rules of transmogrification! You can only hold that form a day or two, at most."

"You lie! I don't have to change back."

"Your essence will dissipate. You won't be yourself anymore, you'll be—"

"An actual bat!"

Grackle buried his face in his hands. "This is literally the stupidest response possible."

"You've seen nothing yet."

Another flash, another cloud of smoke. Kevin was now two bats.

"Gaius, what you're attempting—it's like a human trying to drown themselves in an inch of water. Your reflexes won't let you, you'll change back. You don't have the will."

"See if I don't!"

Flash, flash, poof! Again Kevin doubled and redoubled. Bats fluttered in a small swarm around Grackle.

"Imbecile. Cut that out! The more forms you manifest, the shorter your time."

"Is that so," the voice replied dryly. Flash, poof. "I will escape this battle and live forever. As bats. Tons of them!"

Flash. Nocturnal screeching now split the sky. Flash, flash again. More than a hundred fruit bats now swooped and rose around Grackle.

"At your current rate, you'll be dead in minutes. Stop this lunacy."

"I won't. I won't leave this church. I'll live in the belfry. I'll live in *all* the belfries."

"Gaius. Kevin, please. You don't have to do this. Come down and we'll discuss it."

The light from the fissions lit the distant hills. The beating of thousands of wings rustled the treetops in a growling cyclone. In its midst, a concussive howl rose up grumbling from the earth, shaking the headstones, threatening the stars above.

"Kevin. Damn you, you're coming apart!"

Driven by a single force, the cloud of bats rose sharply, shrieking skyward in what looked like a concerted effort to spell out something against the stars. Letters took shape but words failed to form. Then silence. As if suddenly released, the swarm dove, scouring out over the earth in a rush of flight—up into the hills, over the nearby wood, through the sleeping town. When the spur of their momentum had spent, they circled back. The conflux swirled once, twice, before slowly frittering away.

Grackle stood motionless in the churchyard, uselessly surveying the barren night sky.

10. The Aftermath

VAMPIRE HUNTER IN TOWN, the *Husker* had reported. *Undead be on guard!*

His footsteps echoing on the marble tile, the supernatural exterminator known to mortals as Edvard von Heusen once again traversed the center aisle of St. Agnew's Church. Once again upon reaching the altar, he stooped to one knee. Here, he decided, he would set the scene for his confrontation with the monster. The churchyard might have offered a more dramatic setting, but indoors no one was likely to interrupt his work.

Removing the string of garlic from his neck, he

slashed a few bulbs with his claws, grinding the rest beneath his boot.

Next, with a running jump, he hurled his body into a set of pews, shattering them three rows deep.

That accomplished, Grackle approached the altar. A single, focused blow from his fist cracked it roughly in two, a jagged cleft down the middle. He hoped to suggest the stone table from *The Lion, the Witch and the Wardrobe:* magic working backward, evil undone. Just two small drops of blood upon the altar cloth, a nice touch.

Grackle took deep satisfaction in this part of the job, the craftsmanship of it. Implying violence where none had been necessary.

Next, he turned to the statuary in the alcoves. Kevin had done some inspired colorwork here, using only nail polish. In the complexion of St. Sebastian's face, the anguish from the arrow wounds mixed deliciously with the ecstasy of suffering in his master's name. This artistic desecration must have made the young vampire feel like he was pissing his time away, but he really had a skill. What a pity.

With an implacable hand, he crushed the marvelous visage to dust.

Eddie van Housing. Kevin had gotten the joke. Grackle had worried it might have been a touch too subtle.

He lifted his eyes upward. The crucifix or no? Either the roosting vampire had mutilated it in his agony, or the transfixed messiah had watched the fight between good and evil with tranquil indifference. Which would evoke the better horror in the minds of the townsfolk?

The Christ gave him a little wink.

The hunter left it.

No vampire may kill another without a writ from the Council.

Grackle removed a scroll from the lining of his cloak and lay it flat upon the broken altar. Using a notched thumbnail to open a vein in his wrist, Grackle bloodied the letters GAIUS SEVERUS on the line naming the proscribed. Down below where a signature was required, he scratched GRACULUS ATROX, C.O.A.

Offense? Oh, anything. POOR DENTAL HYGIENE.

All that was left was the seal. Damn it, which pocket was it in?

Grackle was surprised Kevin hadn't become suspicious when he claimed to have watched the Council carefully for centuries. It was a poorly kept secret that most of what the vampires knew of the Council was little more than theater. Everything about that body, including its membership, was clandestine.

Some of the Council members have been jealously guarding their power for five millennia, they can't wait to be dethroned.

Alas, too true. No matter how odious the burden, the spirit refuses to cede place until it encounters a superior. Among humans, sickness and age make this meeting inevitable. But among the undead . . .

For the next master of the world, indifference to pleasure would be a necessary trait. Fearlessness, another. This combination alone could obliterate the ancient powers. Grackle had hoped he would find Kevin nourishing a purer will. Unfortunately, Grackle had found nothing more than the will to die.

"I was offering you ultimate dominion," he mused, "but you made me into a giver of mercies."

A vampire as young as Quercus couldn't generate enough mutagen to turn more than a score of vampires, two if he was particularly virile. The consequence he'd face from his corporate masters for this limited production would be unenviable. A financial asset now, he'd remain an item on a balance sheet, sold and transferred dozens of times while he molded away in storage. Yet escape would be the last thing he'd attempt: Quercus knew that whatever agony and indignity he endured at the hands of the humans, he still awaited trial before the vampires. The sentence would be brutal. It would not be death.

Quercus was going nowhere. That was satisfactory for now.

But the vampires made from harvesting him would probably need to be destroyed. Billionaires wedded to their business enterprises, terminally ill children of parents too weak-willed to endure the loss, Hollywood stars terrified of aging. Immortality was not for them. But Grackle would watch them for half a century, perhaps. Who knows, sometimes people surprise you.

The moon had begun to rise over the churchyard. A fetid wind scattered the clouds and the stars came out.

Grackle jumped down into Kevin's grave, hauled the coffin aboveground, and carried it into the church. He set it down before the altar, where it'd be the first thing the mortals saw. It didn't make much sense, but without a body, you needed a casket. Grackle laid a spare cloak from his duffel bag neatly inside the lining. Drawing the pouch of funerary ash from his belt, he poured a trickle down the center of the fabric, heavier mounds where the head and heart might have been.

Don't create a forensic masterpiece, he thought. *Just enough so the townies can believe whatever they want.*

Vampire hunting runs in families for a reason. Every generation or so you've got to change your name, modify your appearance.

Don't you recognize an old friend, Gaius? It's me, Grackle.

Inertia and indolence. If only. For the true masters of the world, maintaining the balance was an endless process. The tree of immortality required you to clip every unnecessary leaf and bud. Eternal life was far more fragile than most imagined.

How hard to make unending life livable! Every recess of knowledge and experience needed to be explored, not for edification but survival. Become intimate with the earth, all the natural and man-made phenomena upon it. Study each science, immerse yourself in every culture, stand with your own feet upon the heights and depths and the unreachable perches. Or perish.

As Grackle turned to leave the chapel, he looked up at the mural of the Assumption of Mary. *Put your back into it! Heave!* Yes, ye Cath-o-licks, you understand it. It sure takes a lot of work.

Grackle threw open the double doors at the front of the church. Pausing briefly before the threshold, he took a long ceremonial step out into the night air. Another job completed.

To the east, he saw the horizon beginning to lighten. Many miles yet to a secure crypt where he could wait out the day. He didn't have much time.

But enough. Ye brutal gods, always more than enough.

ACKNOWLEDGMENTS

I'd like to offer the following thanks: To Robert Crow, Holly Hollar, Nikki Nelson-Hicks, Marc Taurisano, Jay Traub, and Emily Weaver, for their feedback on this story. Each made a significant contribution to the final outcome. To Emily again, for subjecting herself to multiple versions of this story, and for believing this book should exist in the first place. To Keri Knutson, for ingenious use of corn in the cover art. And finally, to Maegan Black, for naming Kevin's nail polish. Even if she only meant it as a joke, I couldn't imagine not making her a part of this. I miss you, my friend.